SHIN
AND THE CHAO
CREW

The Day of the GREAT CHASE

Written by Chris Callaghan and Zoë Clarke

Illustrated by Amit Tayal

Collins

Shinoy and the Chaos Crew

When Shinoy downloads the Chaos Crew app on his phone, a glitch in the system gives him the power to summon his TV heroes into his world.

With the team on board, Shinoy can figure out what dastardly plans the red-eyed S.N.A.I.R., a Super Nasty Artificial Intelligent Robot, has come up with, and save the day.

"It looks wonky," Shinoy said, angling his head.

Toby wheeled the go-kart around Shinoy's driveway. "It'll be fine."

Myra appeared. "What's that?"

"A go-kart. Obviously," Shinoy said. "We're entering the annual Flat Hill go-kart race."

"Hmm," Myra said. "It looks wonky."

"Are you coming to watch?" Toby asked.

"Nope. Dad's taking me to a Maths conference!"

"Helmets, arm pads, kneepads ..."

"*Muuum*! We're going to be late," Shinoy harrumphed.

"Safety first, boys!" Mum said. "If you steer the go-kart into a ditch, you'll be protected."

"Thanks!" Shinoy said.

Toby and Shinoy ran off up the road, pulling the go-kart behind them. Dad drove by in his brown Relic 500, honking the horn. Myra leaned out of the window and shouted, "Good luck!"

Shinoy pinned the number 5 to the go-kart.

"They give us a gentle push and off we go, right?" Toby asked.

"Yup. We go in two-minute intervals. Everyone gets an individual time, and the quickest to the finish is the winner."

"We're not going to win, are we?"

Shinoy shook his head. "Don't think so. But it'll be fun to take part."

The countdown began: "3-**2**-**1** ..." and they were off.

"That was not a gentle push!" Toby squeaked, as the go-kart set off super speedily. "And that official had weird red eyes, like S.N.A.I.R.!"

As they rounded the first bend, Shinoy felt a weight on the back of the go-kart. He turned to find Merit hanging on to the back.

"Shinoy!" Merit gave a cheery wave. "I'm on a skateboard!"

"How did you get here?" Shinoy shouted back at him.

"Didn't you put out a Chaos Crew call?"

"Nope. My phone's in my pocket."

"Bet you activated the app with your bottom," Toby laughed.

"Where did you get the skateboard?" Shinoy asked.

"I borrowed it. I calculated it would be the best mode of transport to catch you up."

"Lean left!" Shinoy said, as they rounded another bend.

"What's *this* contraption you're in?" Merit asked.

"It's a go-kart. We made it from bits of wood," Toby said, proudly. "We're in a race!"

Merit pulled a face. "Hmm. It looks wonky. It's steering way too far to the right."

Just at the point the go-kart should have gone left towards the finish, it crashed through the straw bales and bounced off to the right.

"We seem to be picking up speed," Merit observed.

"Hold on tight," Shinoy yelled.

"I'm not sure how to stop!"

The go-kart squelched through the bottom of the field and straight on to the second steepest hill in Flat Hill. The one with the cobbles.

"It's going to get a bit bumpy!" Shinoy yelled.

"I am not enjoying this anymore!"

Toby held his hands
in front of his eyes.
"I'm not looking."

"Where's your sense
of adventure?"
Merit grinned. "Your spirit
of discovery, your – *oooh*, that's
not good."

"What?" Toby yelped,
peering through
his fingers.

"Hedge!"

W - h - o - o - m - p - h!

"Washing line!"

"*Ahhhhhhhhhhhh!*"

"What we need," Merit shouted, "is more speed!"

Shinoy shook his head. "No! That's not what we need."

They whizzed down a narrow street. One of the back wheels came flying off.

"Look!" Toby pointed. "It's Myra and your dad!"

They were standing by the roadside, looking miserable. Smoke was pouring out of the Relic 500.

Merit put one foot down and dug his heel into the ground. The road rippled under his feet like a carpet as the go-kart came to a halt.

"Why didn't you do that before?" Shinoy asked.

Merit looked a bit guilty. "Umm. I was having fun ..."

They rolled up to Dad and Myra.

"What's happened?" Shinoy asked.

"It's blown a gasket," Dad said. "We're not going to get to the conference."

Shinoy started to laugh, but then he saw Myra's face. Just because he thought a Maths conference was boring, that didn't mean she did.

He looked at Merit. “When you said that we need more speed, did you mean you’ve got a gadget for that?”

Merit whipped out a metal box with rotor blades. “I happen to have a one-shot-hits-the-spot Turbo Enhancer.”

Toby held out his hands. “Wow! We can attach this to the go-kart and still win – even with three wheels.”

"Or," Shinoy said, "we can attach it to the Relic 500 and get Myra and Dad to the conference."

"*Then* we can attach it to the go-kart," Toby said.

Merit shook his head. "One-shot only, amigo. You can only use it once."

"What? Then it explodes in a ball of electric flame?" Toby asked.

"No. Then you have to change the batteries," Merit said. "And I don't have spares."

Shinoy didn't hesitate. "Put it on the Relic."

"Anything for you, Shinoy." Merit smiled. "And the lovely Myra."

Myra pulled a face, but Shinoy could see she was smiling.

Once the Turbo Enhancer was attached to the car, the Relic 500 trundled off.

"Let's get back to the course," Shinoy said, dragging the go-kart.

Back at the finish line, the prizes were being presented.

"The prize for the go-kart least likely to finish the course goes to … ah … *here* they are! Number 5 driven by Shinoy, Toby and … ?"

"Merit," Shinoy shouted.

"… and Derek!"

"We've won a wheel attached to a piece of wood," Merit said.

Shinoy grinned.
"We do need a wheel.
Come on, *Derek*, Let's fix it
to the go-kart and have one last ride."

Off-road map

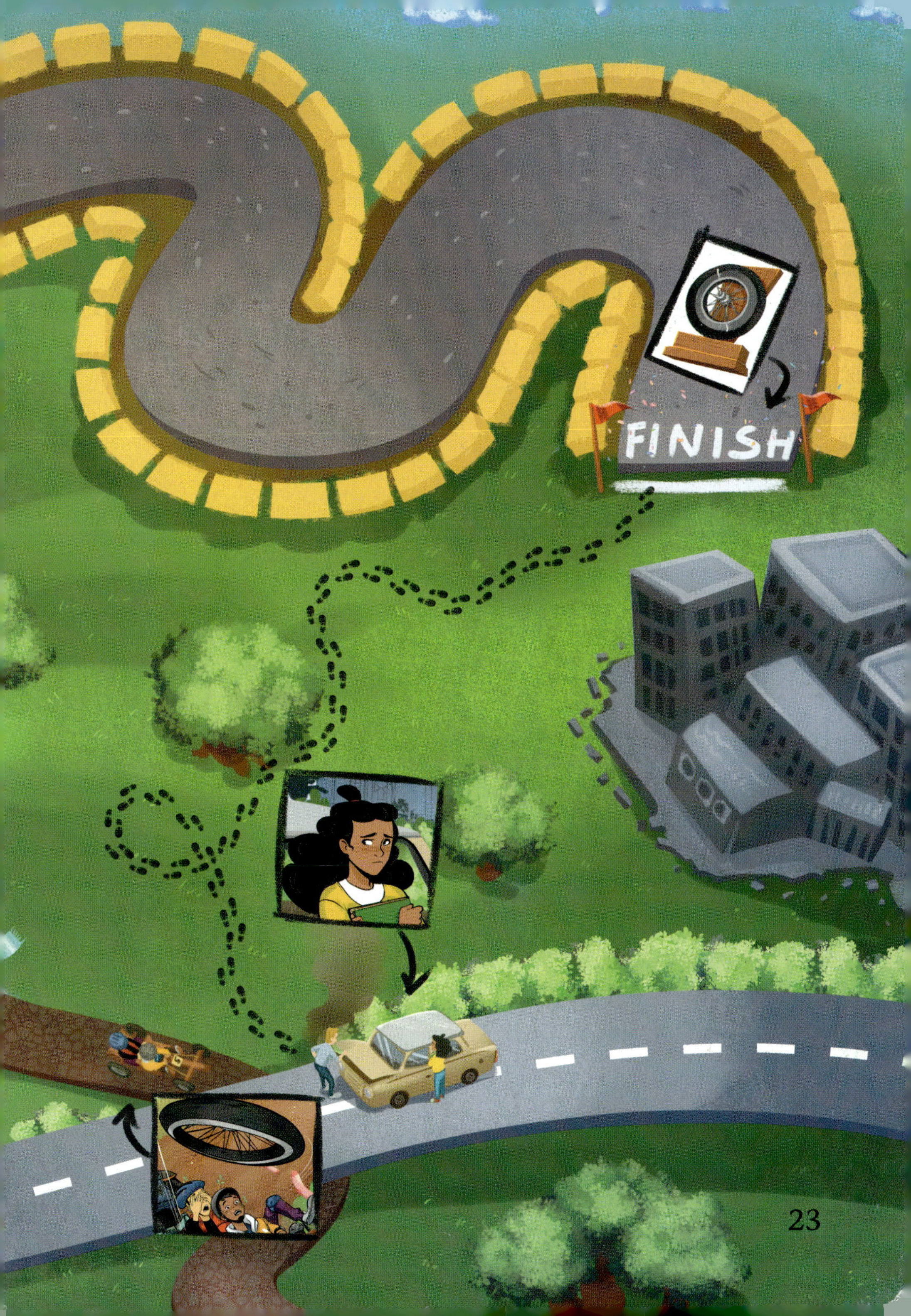
FINISH

Ideas for reading

Written by Clare Dowdall, PhD
Lecturer and Primary Literacy Consultant

Reading objectives

- discuss the sequence of events in books and how items of information are related
- discuss their favourite words and phrases
- draw on what they already know or on background information and vocabulary provided by the teacher
- make inferences on the basis of what is being said and done

Spoken language objectives

- use relevant strategies to build their vocabulary
- give well-structured descriptions and explanations
- use spoken language to develop understanding through speculating, hypothesising, imagining and exploring ideas

Curriculum links: Science – working scientifically; Design technology – design, make, evaluate; PSHE – health and wellbeing: feelings

Word count: 964

Interest words: mode of transport, sense of adventure, spirit of discovery, one-spot-hits-the-spot Turbo Enhancer, ball of electric flame

Resources: paper and pencils, construction materials, tape measure/ meter-ruler

Build a context for reading

- Look at the front cover together and read the title *The Day of the Great Chase*. Ask children to describe what they can see and explain what they think is happening, and what is going to happen in the story.
- Ask a volunteer to read the back cover blurb to the group. Ask for any examples of when children have been in runaway vehicles (scooters, rollerskates, bicycles, go-karts).
- Make a list of adjectives that describe how Shinoy might be feeling in the runaway go-kart, based on the children's own experiences.